The Fellowship of the Noodle: The Journey Begins

by Evelyn & Alexander Fuchs

illustrated by Aspen Layer

Love It Publishing

LOVE IT PUBLISHING

Published by Love It Publishing, LLC (USA)

www.LoveItPublishing.com

Love It Publishing
ISBN-10: 0-9983801-1-3   ISBN-13: 978-0-9983801-1-7

Dedicated to our awesome team, the JP2 Rockslides,
and everyone who taught us the value of teamwork

One day, as he was flying along, a fly saw a noodle and thought to himself: Hey look! A delicious noodle! I'll try to bring it to that hill over there so I can enjoy it in peace.

4

The fly went down,
      and pushed,
         and pulled,
            and flew with all his might...

...but it was so heavy, the noodle only moved a little.

The fly sat down to rest and noticed an ant looking for food. So the fly called out,
"Hey Mr. Ant!
Will you help me move this noodle up the hill?"

The ant considered this idea and responded,
"Sure! If I can have some when we're done."

The fly nodded, so the ant came over to help.

Together, the ant and the fly pushed,

and pulled,

and flew,

and crawled,

with all their might...

...but the noodle only moved a little.

As they paused, they saw a moth fluttering above them.

So they shouted, "HELP!"

When the moth came down, they explained what they wanted to do and he agreed to help.

Together, they pushed,
and pulled,
and flew,
and crawled,
and fluttered,

with all their might...

...but the noodle only moved a little.

When they stopped, they
saw a dragonfly zooming
over them.

So they yelled, "HELP!"
with all their might.

Then the dragonfly swooped down...

and ate the moth.

"Hey! Why did you do that?!" scolded the fly.

Quickly, the dragonfly spit out the moth. "I thought that's what you meant by helping....He looked like he was bothering you!" the dragonfly reasoned.

PTOOEY

The moth flew away yelling,
    "Fly for your lives!"

11

"Well, could *you* help us carry this noodle?" the ant questioned.

"Sure," the dragonfly replied.

Together they pushed,
       and pulled,
              and flew,
       and crawled,
       and buzzed,

with all their might...

...but the noodle only moved a little.

As they puffed, they saw a grasshopper in the distance, so they hollered, "Will you come and help us carry this noodle?"

The grasshopper came right over to help them.

Together they pushed,
  and pulled,
    and flew,
      and crawled,
        and buzzed,
          and hopped,
with all their might...

...but the noodle *still* only moved a little.

"Okay, clearly this isn't working,"
wheezed the fly. "We need a plan."

The ant suggested, "What if we called an armadillo?"

"Don't you remember what happened with the moth?" the fly reminded him.

"And where would we find an armadillo?" questioned the grasshopper.

munch, munch, munch, munch...

18

"Hey! What are you doing?" fumed the fly, "We're supposed to eat that later!"

"*Cuál es tu problema?*" the caterpillar asked.

"*...What?...*" they all blurted.

"**What is your problem?**" asked the suave caterpillar.

20

"We want to move this noodle up the hill, but it's too heavy," complained the fly.

"You need to work together," answered the caterpillar, "What we need is a team building exercise. Does anybody have a hula hoop?"

The ant replied, "I left mine at home. Do you want me to go get it?"

21

"That will not be necessary," the caterpillar continued, "We'll do without.

I have a plan.

Ant and I are good at crawling. We'll take up the front.

Dragonfly and Fly, you have good eyesight and can fly, you'll be behind us keeping watch. Grasshopper, you take up the rear."

22

"Wait!" the fly suggested, "Your idea gave me an idea!

What if Grasshopper is in between Dragonfly and I, to make sure the noodle doesn't sag, and Ant is at the end?"

= BIGGER YAY

"You're right, that's a great suggestion!" said the caterpillar. Everyone agreed.

23

Together they pushed, and pulled,

and flew, and crawled,

and buzzed, and hopped,

and skittered,

with all their might...

...and the noodle started moving
toward the top of the hill!

"We're doing it!" whooped the excited grasshopper.

Once they got the noodle up the hill, they all rested for a while, and then started eating.

Except the dragonfly, who said he wanted something more filling.

When they were done, the dragonfly suggested, "We should form a team in case something like this happens again."

"Yes," agreed the caterpillar, "We will become...La Alianza de los Fideos!"

"A mariachi band?" asked the ant.

"No, but that's not a bad idea."

"The Fellowship of the Noodle!" exclaimed the caterpillar.

28

"Where did the mantis come from?" asked the fly.

"A mariachi band," the mantis replied.

"Yes!!" cried the ant.

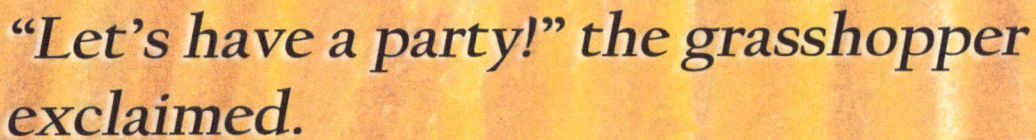

"Let's have a party!" the grasshopper exclaimed.

"I brought maracas!" the ant shouted.

And that is how the journey began.

30

Working as a team is great in everyday life. Try this noodle teamwork game with your friends. Which way works the best?

Supplies:
A play tunnel, bean bags, 5 friends

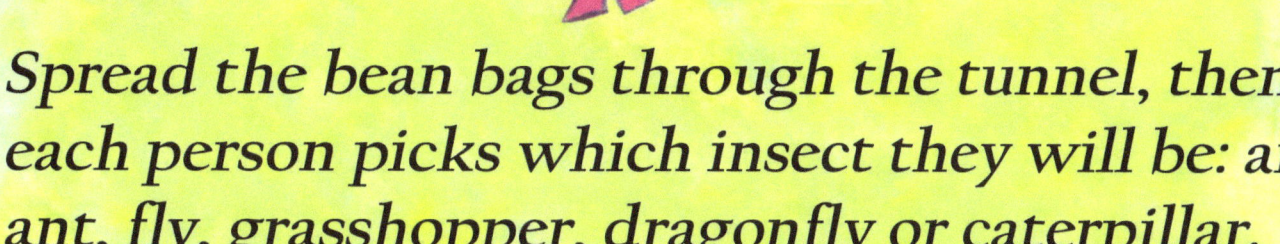

Spread the bean bags through the tunnel, then each person picks which insect they will be: an ant, fly, grasshopper, dragonfly or caterpillar. Arrange yourselves along the tunnel and carry it like the noodle using your insect ability. The tunnel cannot touch the ground and the bean bags can't spill out. How well can you work together as a team?

What are other ways teamwork can help you in everyday life?